This Book Belongs to

For Sue, Thomas and Claire,
and for Molly,
with love
CV

First published in hardback in Great Britain in 2001 by HarperCollins Publishers Ltd
First published in paperback by Collins Picture Books in 2002
Collins Picture Books is an imprint of the Children's Division, part of HarperCollins Publishers Ltd

Text and illustrations copyright © Clara Vulliamy 2001
1 3 5 7 9 10 8 6 4 2
ISBN: 978-0-00-784674-0

The HarperCollins website address is: www.harpercollins.co.uk

Printed in China

Small

Clara Vulliamy

HarperCollins *Children's Books*

Tom is going to stay the night at Granny's for the very first time.
He finds his little suitcase under the bed.
Tom has a lot of important packing to do.

"I will need
my pens
and my torch,
my red slippers
and my blanket
and my best book
of dinosaurs…

and, of course,
I'll need Small."

The suitcase is now so full,
Tom can't even close the lid.

He takes everything out...

and puts it all back in again...

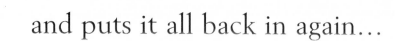

and again…

and again.

At last the suitcase is shut
and Tom is ready to go.

When Tom arrives at Granny's everything is just right.

He has his own toy cupboard
and all his favourite things for tea...

He eats chocolate in the bath
and even bounces on Granny's bed...

There's extra stories at bedtime
and lots of good night kisses.
Tom snuggles down.

BUT...

Suddenly, Tom remembers Small.
"Small?" he whispers.

Small isn't there.

He's not under the pillow, or under the bed...

he's not in the suitcase…

Small must have been left at home!

Tom curls up. He closes his eyes tight and he tries to get to sleep. He thinks about Small, back at home in his bedroom, sad and lonely in the dark.

Small can't sleep either.
"Where's Tom?" he whispers.

He climbs up the curtain.
He squeezes through a tiny gap in the window.

He's down in the street, running...

Small runs and he runs...

He's climbing and tumbling.

And the rain pours down.

And the howling wind pushes him back.

He leaps over puddles.

He trips and falls.

Poor Small.

He's cold and tired
and scared.
But he doesn't stop.
He keeps running and
running, out of the city…

on and on, through the dark, dark woods.

And just when he can bear no more,
Small arrives at Granny's house.

Upstairs, Tom
opens his eyes.

He creeps out of bed.

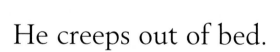

He peeps round the door.
It's all dark and strange.
Tom feels scared,

but he has to find Small.

Ever so quietly he tiptoes
down the stairs. He sees
a light from the kitchen
and he can hear Granny
humming a song.
"Tom, is that you?"
she says.

Step by step he inches
nearer the front door.
And there underneath
the letter box…

...is Small.

Tom scoops him up and hugs him tight.
"You found me!" he says into his chilly, velvety ear.

"He's so small he could have been there all along,"
says Granny as she takes them back to bed.
But Tom doesn't say anything. Tom *knows*.

Now they both know that everything is all right.
And as they snuggle back down in bed, Tom
whispers to Small, "I'll keep you safe forever."

Coming soon…

Meet Tom and Small in their new adventure!

It's the night before Tom's very first day at school and he cannot sleep, but magic is in the air… Join Tom on a midnight adventure in which he shrinks to the size of his toy mouse, Small. Together, they take a ride on the train set, play in the dolls' house and even take to the skies in a model plane.

This story is full of warmth and humour, with a deeply reassuring message about starting school.